I0833193

Printed in the United States of America

First Printing, 2020

ISBN 978-0-9914323-3-2

www.adambotsford.com

Bestiary - Deep Sea Aboleth

Lore: The Aboleth are known for their innate psychic abilities to read the thoughts of those who threaten it and strange poisoned mucus coating that transforms anyone who touches it. The Deep Sea Aboleth offers an even greater threat by using its these two abilities together to turn its victims to temporarily polymorph its victims into the form they or someone nearby fears most. The chaos that ensues is extremely alarming.

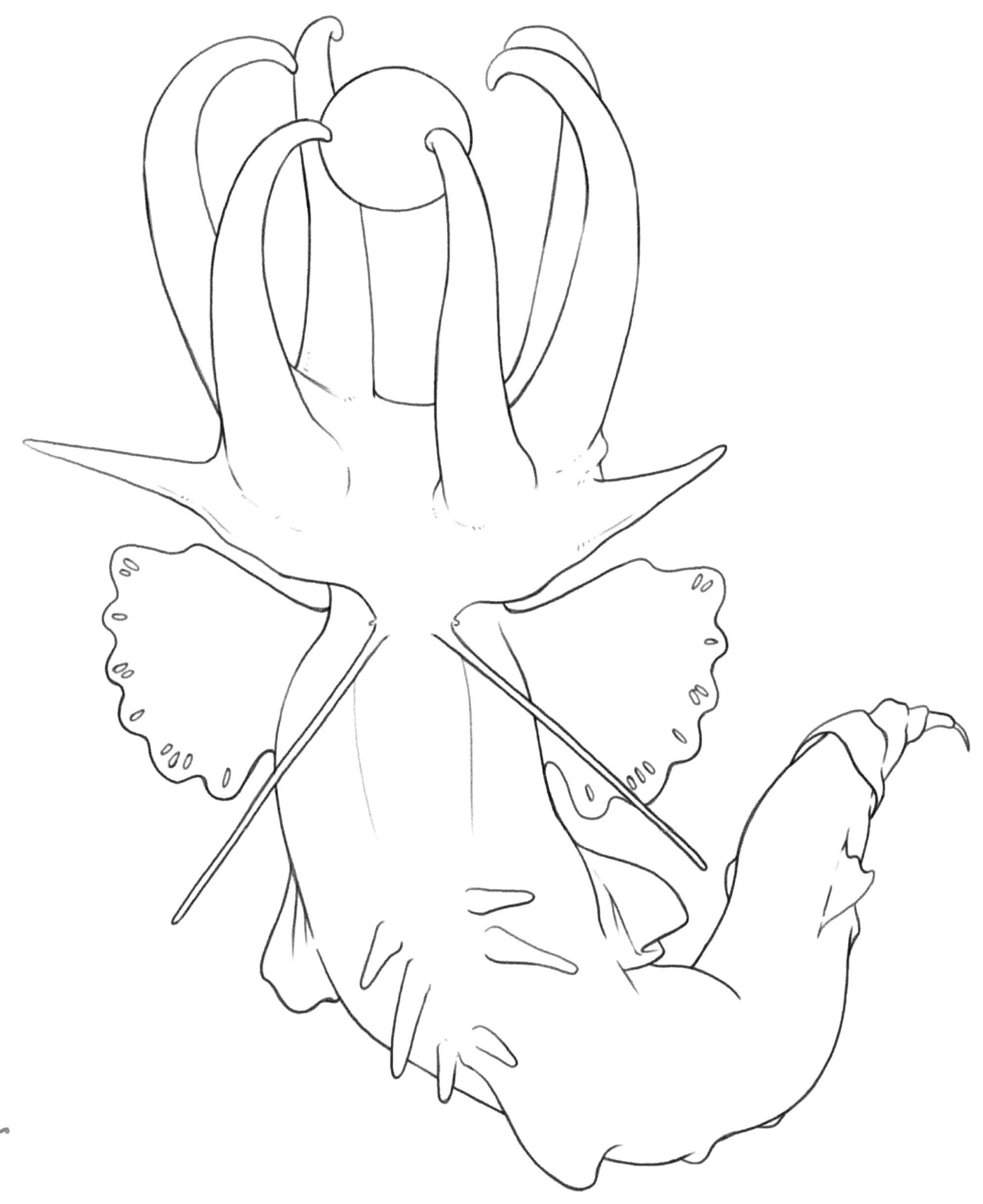

Beast Name: Chimera

Lore:

These creatures are a merger of magic and monsters spawned in places of extreme magical intensity. Casters have recorded incidents of these manifesting spontaneously after a botched spell or as a secondary effect of high-level spells.

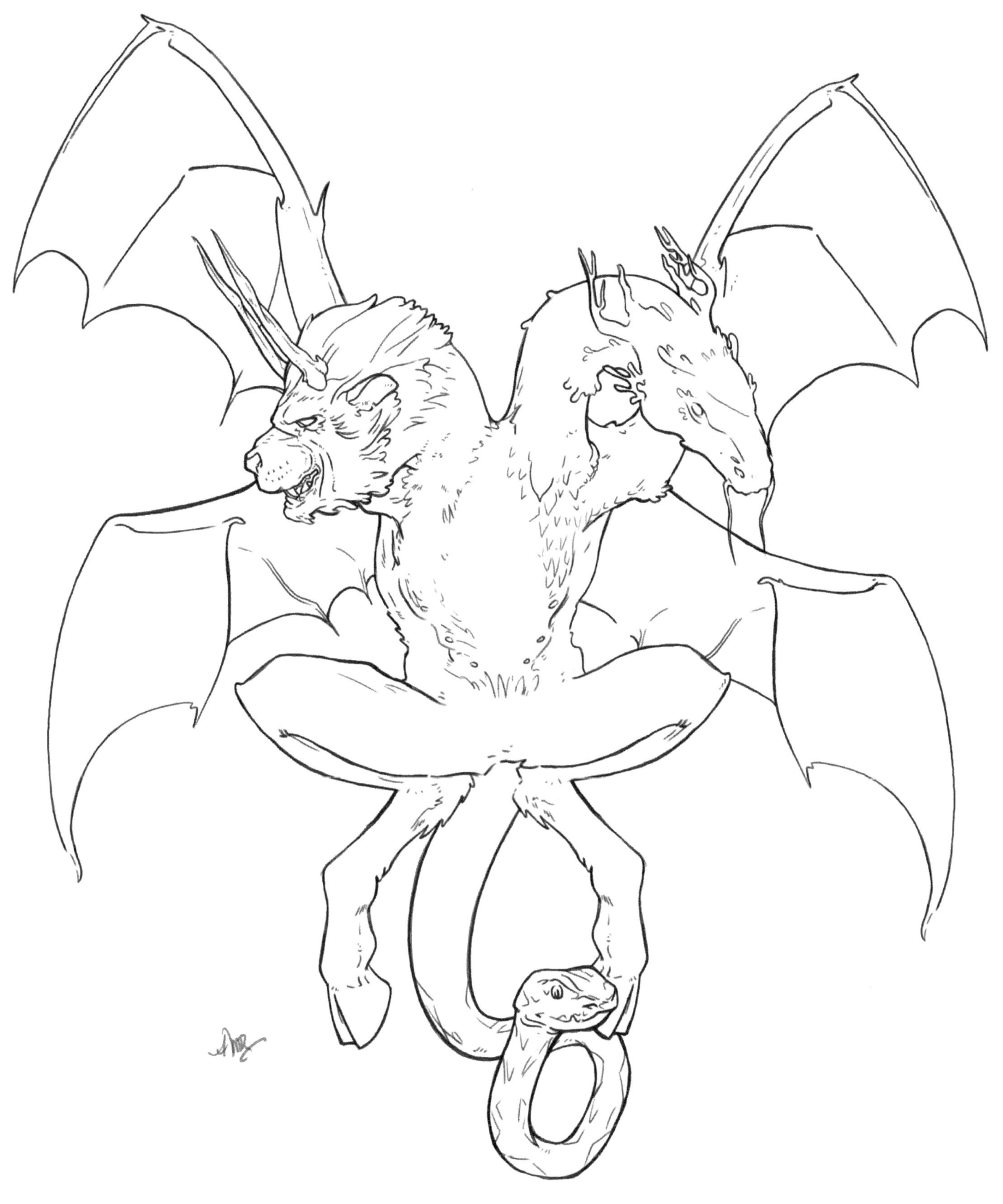

Beast Name: Demon - Discord

Lore:

This demon type resembles a human but features an extra set of arms. They are known to wield staves that are forged from a variety of instruments intended to create discordant sounds. These sounds work like concussive waves and can be used to disrupt sounds at long distances. It's said that the power of this disruption can dissipate a dragon's breath attack or stop a shapeshifter from changing forms. A note of warning for the intrepid group, the Discord demons have an affection for humans and extreme distaste for Genasi.

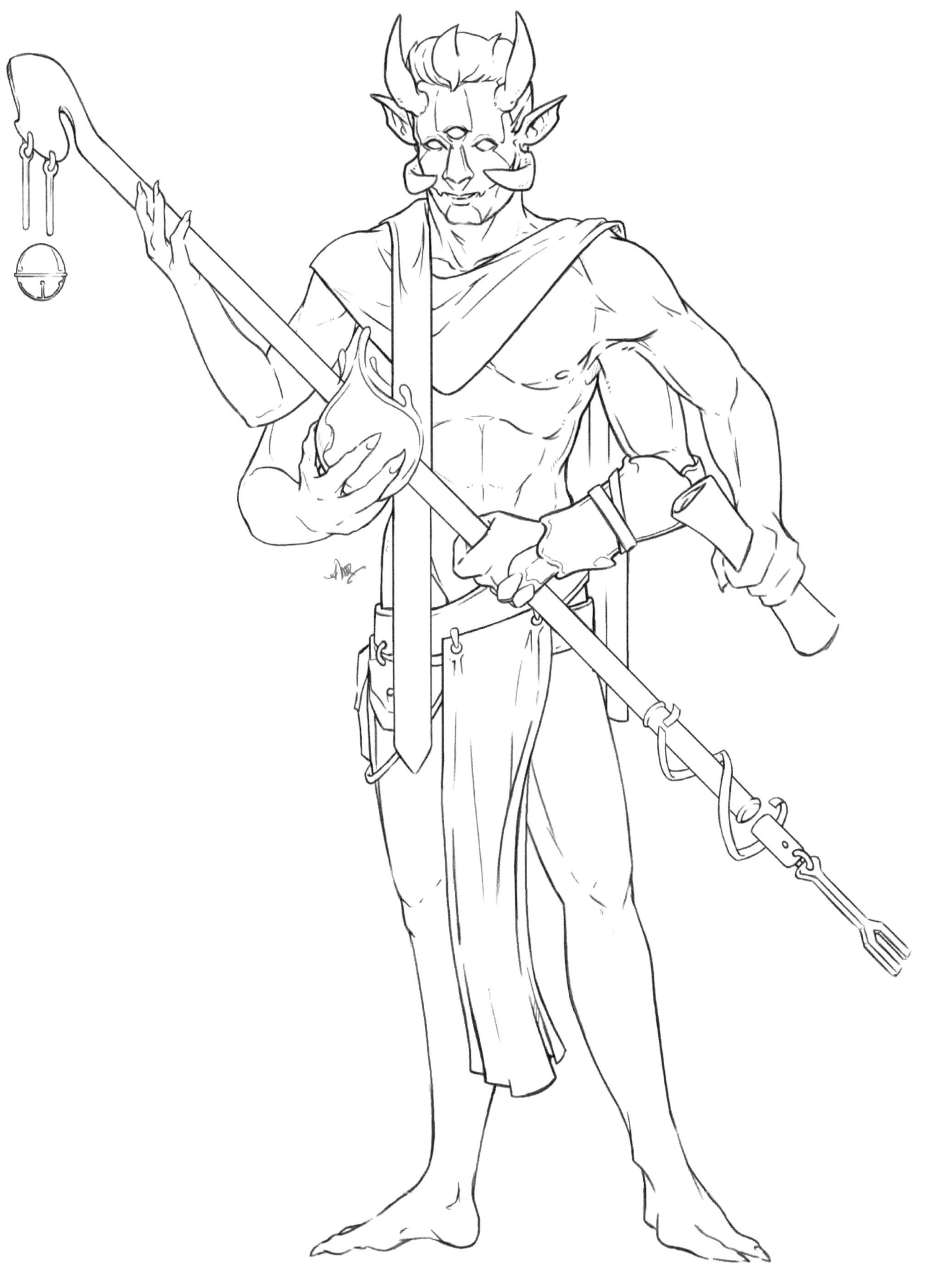

Beast Name: Copper Penny Dragon

Lore:

The Copper Penny Dragon is aptly named for its color and size. Just slightly smaller than a house cat. Like their larger kin, Copper Penny Dragon's live in cities. Their goal is to gather and hoard information. No records exist of their age and it's said that once a great wizard tried to read one's mind only to have her mind ravaged. Her last words were only to speak of seeing all of time and space before going silent forever.

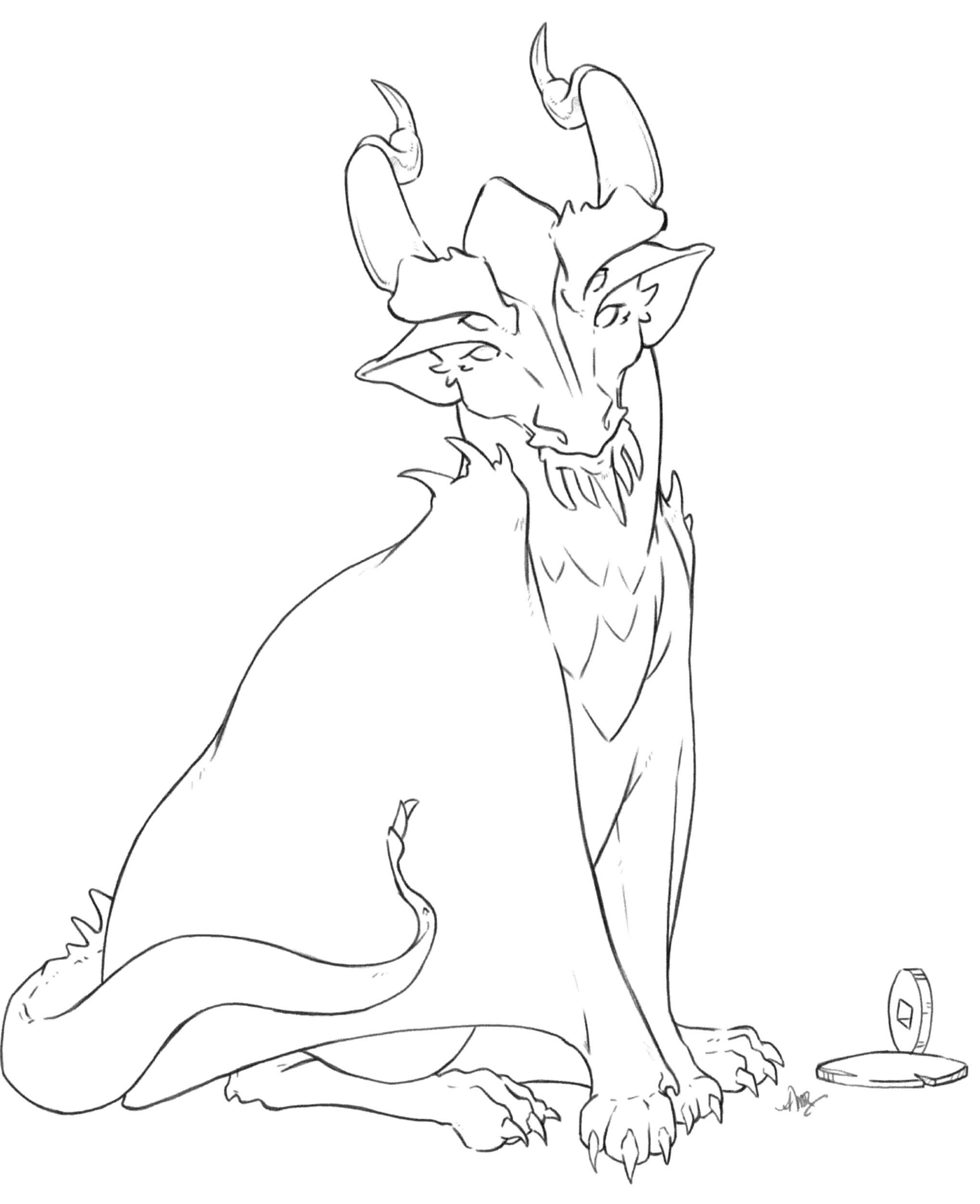

Beast Name: Forest Stalker

Lore:

A distant relative of the cavern dwelling version, these stalkers hide in trees and forest regions using their natural form and magical abilities to hide and wait for unsuspecting adventurers.

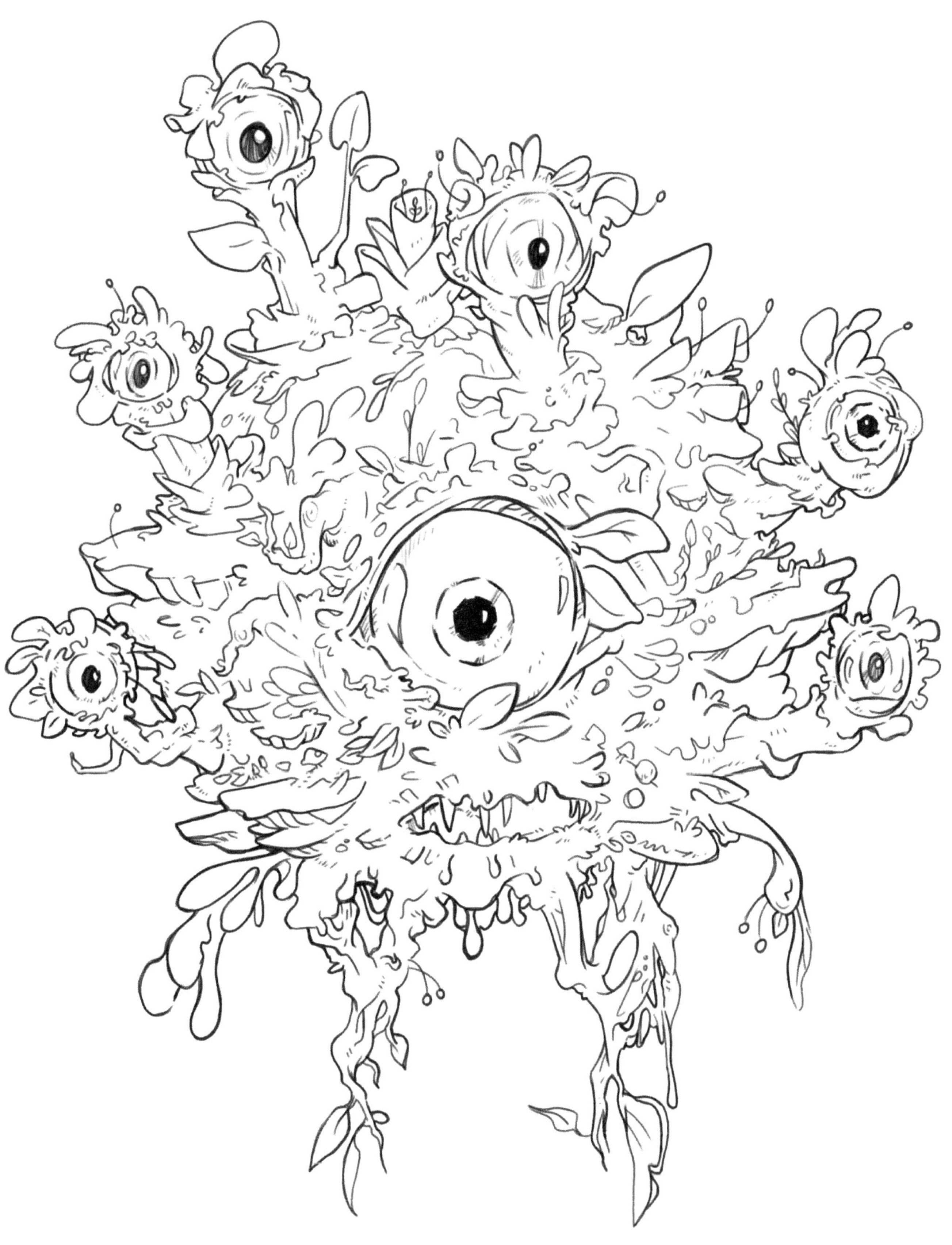

Beast Name: Merkin - Red Shark

Lore:

Merkin are aquatic relatives to merpeople, and make up any variety of partially humanoid water inhabiting creatures. The Red Sharks are known for their psionic abilities. Their name is a misnomer as they are not related to their shark cousins, but instead named after Cyprinidae cousins. Red Shark Merkin average 3ft to 4ft in tail to head length, and are extremely fast swimmers.

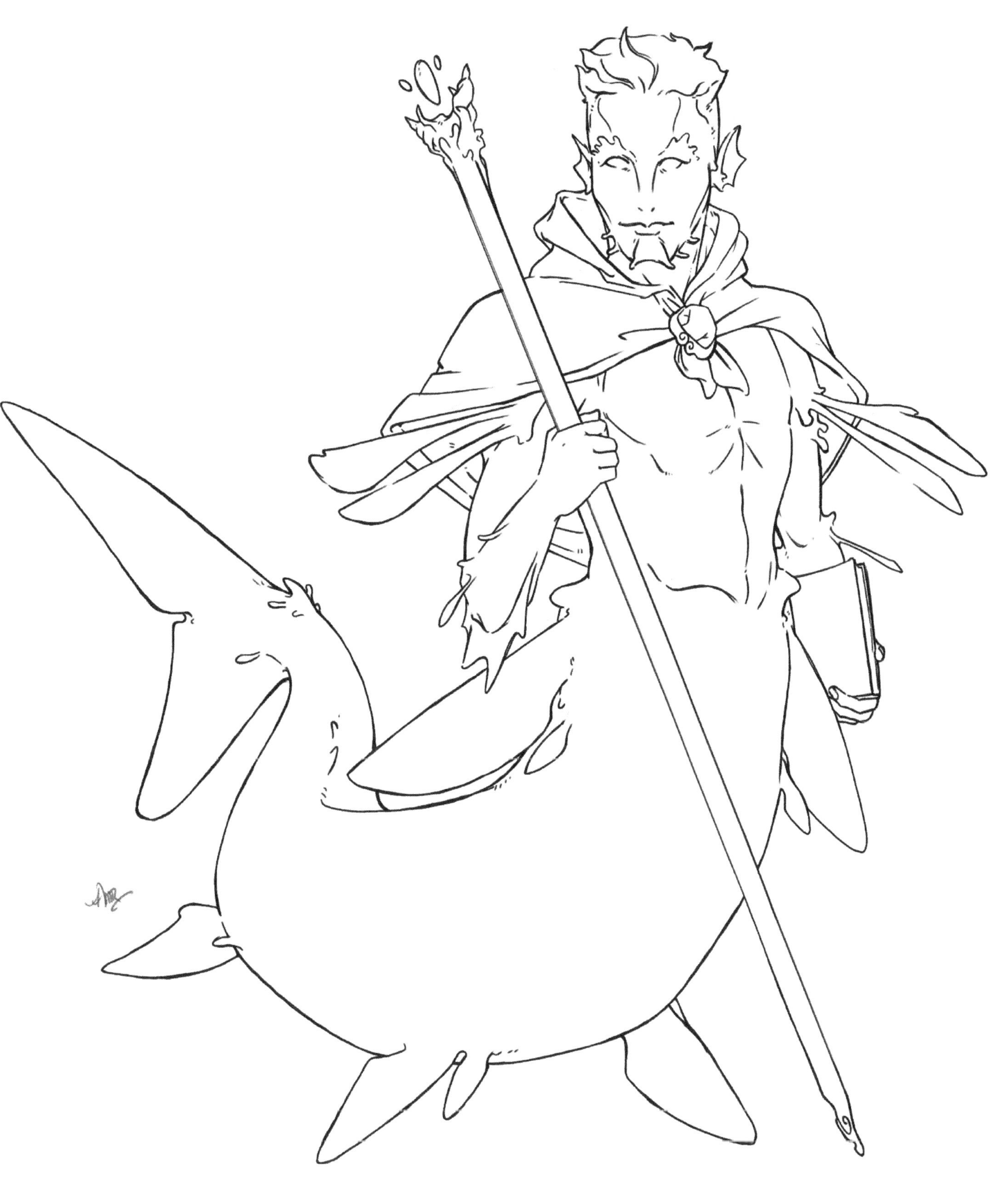

Beast Name: Pandalope

Lore:

Rumored to be of the Kirin family, the Pandalope is just slightly larger than its Red Panda kin. With two sets of horns each containing a set of magical attributes. The horns of the Pandalope are said to vary and can range from a single Unicorn horn to an array or Chromatic dragon spines. Know your taxonomy before engaging. The risk is high.

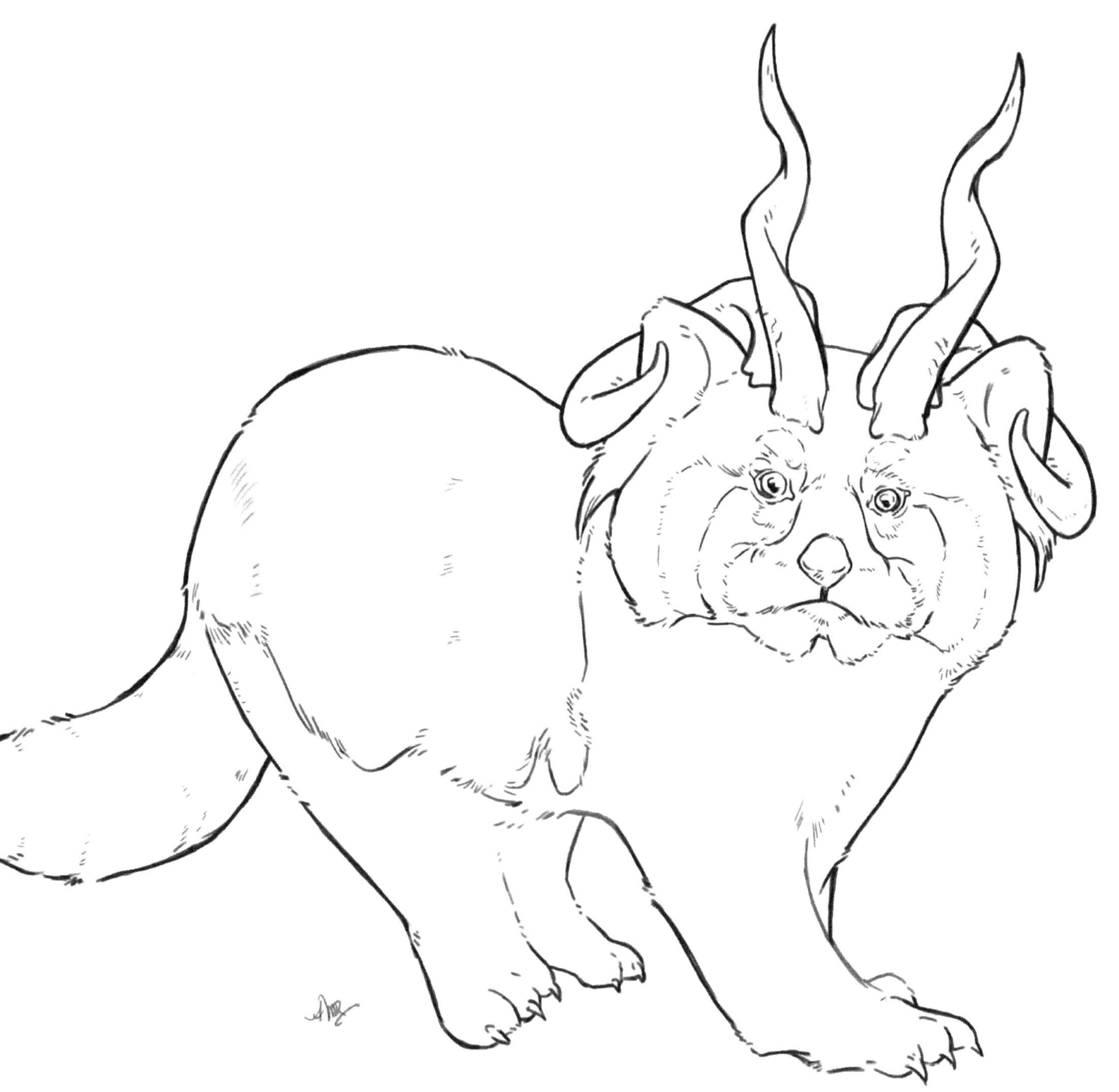

Beast Name: Transient Spiders

Lore:

These spiders are very rare, thankfully so, given their size. Averaging a body length of 2 feet and leg length nearly 3 feet, these creatures are an unwelcome sight by most. Nature saw fit to mark each with intensely bright colors to offer at least one warning of their danger. Their movement is silent. They are capable of shifting planes of existence at will. The only sound they make is that of cracking glass when they shift. One touch can send you, or parts of you, to unknown and unspeakable places.

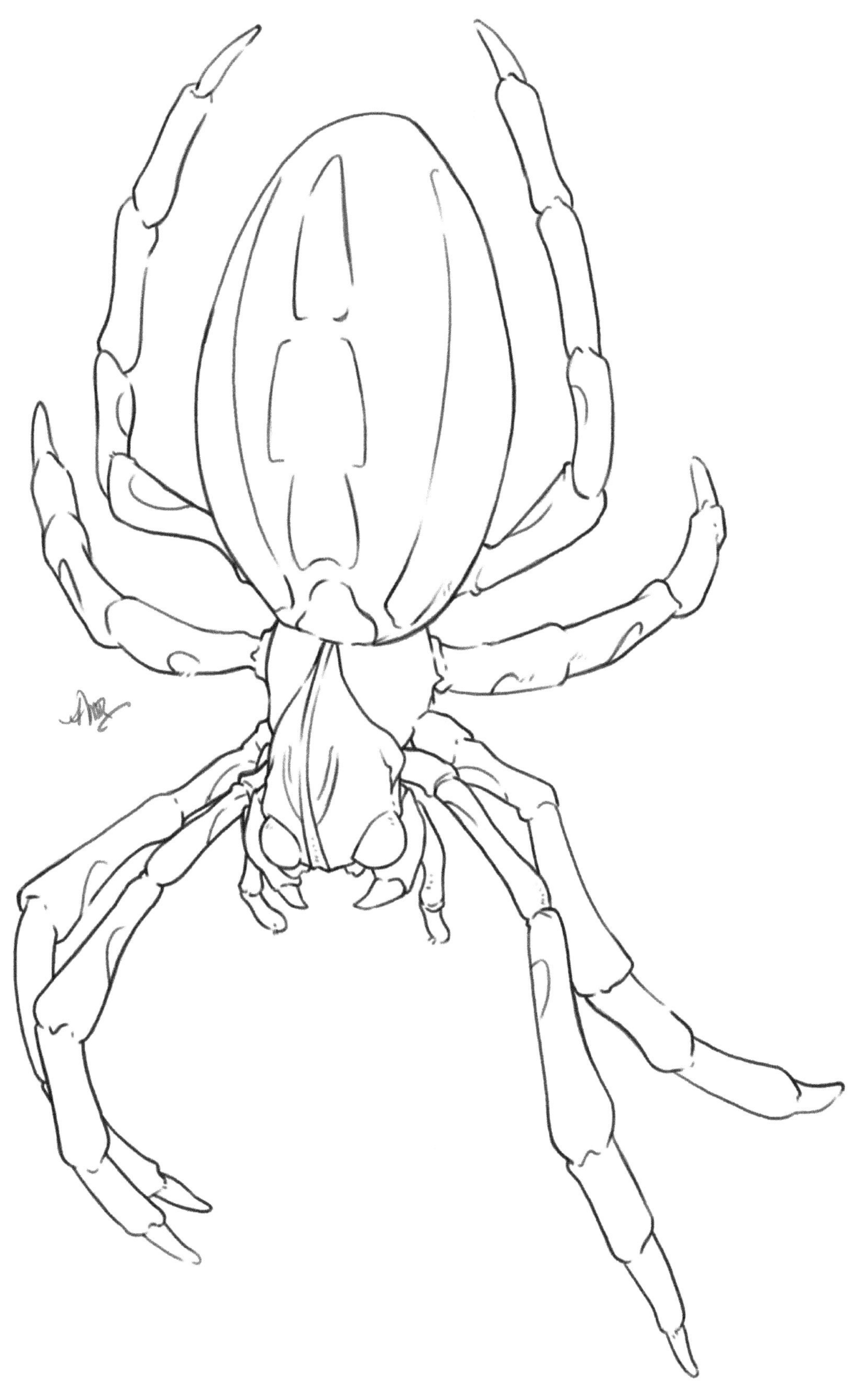

Beast Name: Aquatic Unicorn

Lore:

From deep within the darkest, watery-depths, these unicorns can be found only by the bravest of adventurers. They are not aggressive by nature, but highly territorial and immensely powerful. They control water related magic with more ease than most powerful casters.

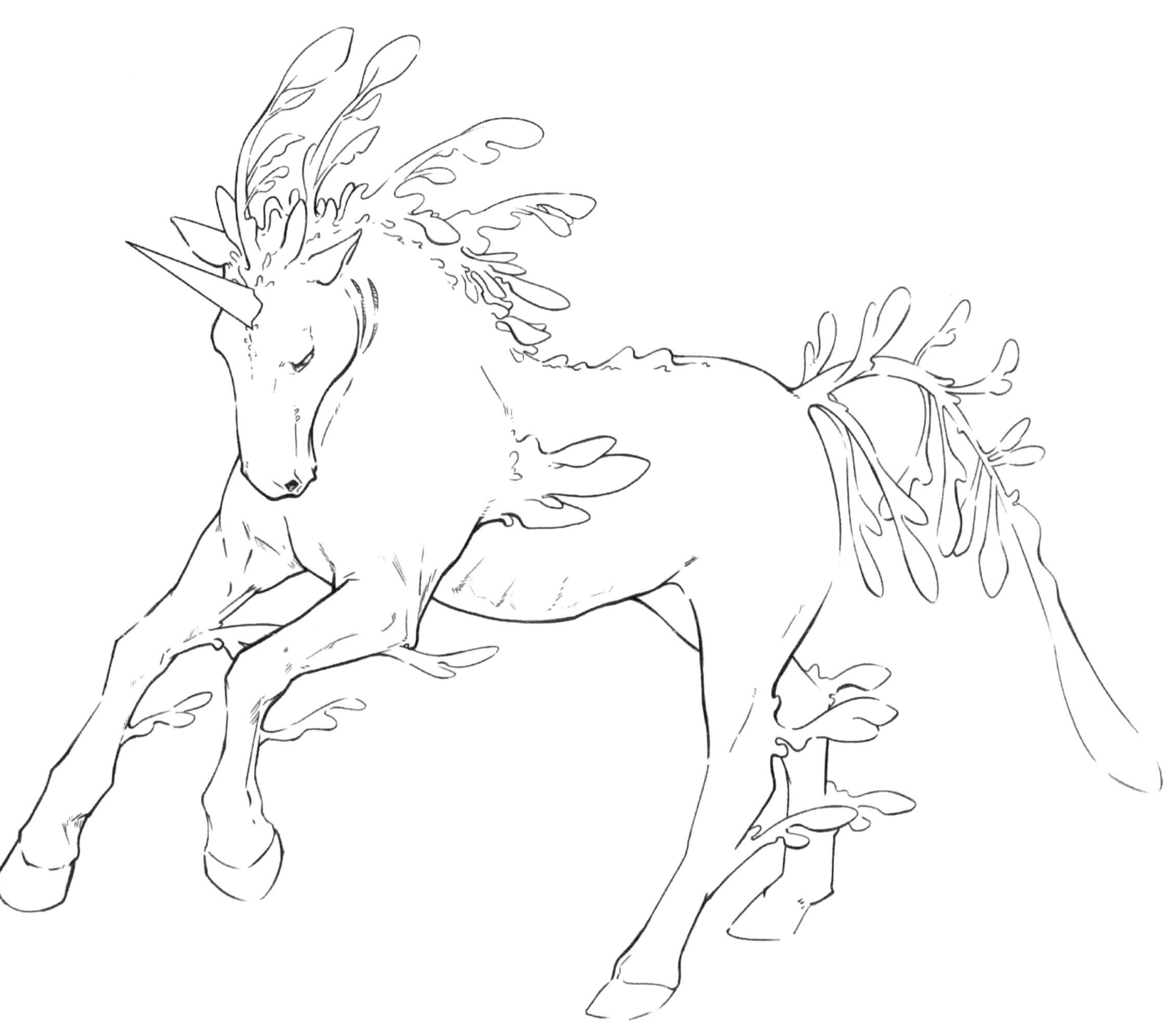

Beast Name: Corrupted Harpy

Lore:

Magical remnants of a great war litter the mountainous terrain these harpies live in. The slow leak of their contained and corrupted magics have leaked into the land and up the food cycle. In this habitat a harpy species was the apex and are still, but time and exposure to the contamination has changed them drastically. Once striking white, these now mottled creatures are fearsome and vicious.

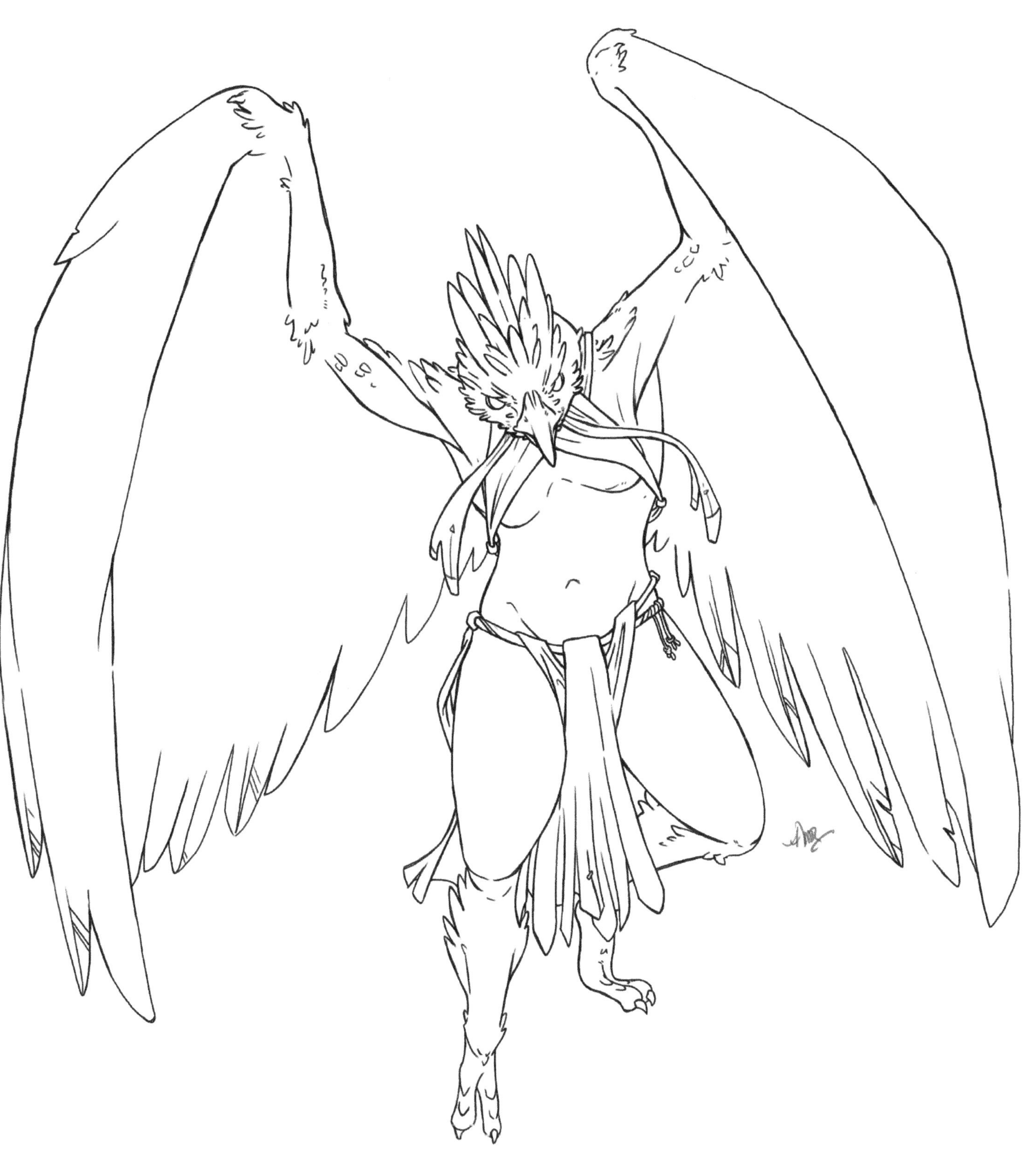

www.ingramcontent.com/pod-product-compliance
Lightning Source LLC
LaVergne TN
LVHW061205120826
845149LV00011B/1918
* 9 7 8 0 9 9 1 4 3 2 3 3 2 *